JACK and JAKE

ALIKI

THE BODLEY HEAD
LONDON

For all the Jacks and Jakes

British Library Cataloguing in Publication Data
Aliki   Jack and Jake.
Rn: Aliki Brandenberg   I. Title
813'.54 [J] PZ7
ISBN 0-370-30727-5

Printed in Great Britain for
The Bodley Head Ltd
30 Bedford Square, London WC1B 3RP
by W.S. Cowell Ltd, Ipswich
First published by Greenwillow Books,
William Morrow and Company, Inc., New York 1986
First published in Great Britain 1986

Why can't they tell Jack from Jake?

They said, "Jack is hungry," when it's Jake who cried.

They said, "Jake is wet," but it's Jack they dried.

They thought Jack was sleepy when Jake yawned and sighed.

What's wrong with them all?

They cooed over Jake when Jack learned how to crawl.

They said, "Jack's first tooth," when Jake started to bawl.

They shouted, "Catch Jake!" when they thought Jack would fall.

Why can't they get them straight?

Jack took his first steps. They said, "Jake can walk."

Jake cried out, "Bow-wow." They said, "Jack can talk."

And guess who they blamed when Jack broke the chalk?

The wrong one, of course.

Jack built a high tower. "Great, Jake," they all said.

Jake wanted more ice cream. Jack got it instead.

Jack sneezed and they cried out, "Put Jake into bed!"

Can't they see?

Jack tried and Jake tried to make them aware.

Jake gave himself freckles. Jack parted his hair.

But poor Jack and poor Jake—they still mixed the pair.

Why don't they look?

Why can't they learn? It's the same old mistake.

It's "Hi, Jake" to Jack and "Goodbye, Jack" to Jake.

"Which one," they whisper, "fell into the lake?"

That did it. I finally told them.

Jack does things and says things that only Jack could.

Jake finds things and likes things that only Jake would.

Jack's Jack and Jake's Jake—is that understood?

It's as simple as that.